COUNTDOWN

COUNTDOWN

M.J. McISAAC

ORCA
ANCHOR

ORCA BOOK PUBLISHERS

Published in Canada and the United States
in 2023 by Orca Book Publishers.
orcabook.com

Library and Archives Canada Cataloguing in Publication
Title: Countdown / M.J. McIsaac.
Names: McIsaac, M. J., 1986- author.
Identifiers: Canadiana (print) 2022018562X |
Canadiana (ebook) 20220185638 |
ISBN 9781459835351 (softcover) | ISBN 9781459835368 (PDF) |
ISBN 9781459835375 (EPUB)
Classification: LCC PS8625.I837 C68 2023 | DDC jC813/.6—dc23

Library of Congress Control Number: 2022934486

Summary: In this high-interest accessible novel for teen readers,
Myles gets a text from someone threatening to expose a dark secret.

Orca Book Publishers is committed to reducing the consumption of
nonrenewable resources in the production of our books. We make
every effort to use materials that support a sustainable future.

Orca Book Publishers gratefully acknowledges the support
for its publishing programs provided by the following agencies:
the Government of Canada, the Canada Council for the Arts and
the Province of British Columbia through the BC Arts Council
and the Book Publishing Tax Credit.

Edited by Tanya Trafford
Design by Ella Collier
Cover photography by Getty Images/Nick Dolding
Author photo by Crystal Jones

Printed and bound in Canada.

26 25 24 23 • 1 2 3 4

Chapter One

Myles, where are you?

School, Mom. Chill.

What, why? Grad isn't for 6 more hours.

I'm not done writing my speech. Wanted to be alone. Too busy at home. Grandma. Pop. Dad. Kate. Need some quiet.

You are at the library?

Bleachers. Wanted fresh air.

How are you writing the speech?

On my phone. Google doc.

I see. How's it going?

It's not.

You can do it, hon. You are the valedictorian!

Ha ha. Don't remind me.

GOOGLE DOCS > VALEDICTORIAN SPEECH

Word Count: 60

Here we are. High school is over. Ninth grade feels so long ago. The question for all of us is, What's next? Some of us will work. Some of us will travel. Some of us are going to schools far away. I was lucky. I got a scholarship to my top university. And it scares me. What if I fail?

Buzz buzz

It's happening.

I'm kinda busy, Jax.

Doing what?

My speech.

Dude. Talk about last minute.

I know. So leave me alone.

OK. BUT I want you to know...Rich Lu's party is ON. Everyone is going.

Everyone? I doubt that.

Gemma's going. If your girlfriend's going, you have to go.

Who said Gemma was going?

Nate.

Oh...well I guess I am going then.

You and me both! Gemma is making

you go. Nate is making me go. We can sulk behind our dates together. It will be great.

Will Lara Moore be there?

Probably. She's besties with Rich.

She hates me.

Lara hates everybody. But who could hate you? You are the golden boy, remember? Top marks. Captain of the rugby team. You're Superman!

Tell that to Lara.

She still mad about the valedictorian thing?

I think so.

How do you know?

Little things. The other day we were

heading into school together. She let the door close on me.

The door?

Yeah.

She probably didn't see you.

I guess.

Forget about Lara. The party will be great.

I hate parties.

Have you heard from Declan lately?

No.

What about Viraj?

NO. I don't talk to them. I don't talk to Declan. I don't talk to Viraj. I don't talk to Mike. I don't WANT to talk to them. Stop asking.

OK. Jeez. Sorry.

I have to work on my speech.

OK. Later, bud.

———

Rich Lu's party?

Hey, babe.

Were you going to tell me?

I wanted it to be a surprise!

You know I don't like parties, Gemma.

You do like parties.

I really don't.

Myles, you are the valedictorian.

Everybody wants you to be there.

I don't care what everybody wants.

What about what I want?

You really want to go?

I really do. I promise it will be fun.

You can't promise that.

Oh yes I can. Trust me. I bought a new top I think you'll love.

Oh yeah?

It's your favorite color, green. And low cut. Like...really low. 😉

Oh. Yeah. 😍

Trust me, babe. It's going to be the night of our lives.

I trust you.

How's the speech coming?

Terrible. I'm never going to finish it.

Yeah, you will. You always find a way.

Thanks, Gem.

Love you 🖤

🖤

GOOGLE DOCS > VALEDICTORIAN SPEECH

Word Count: 66

Here we are. High school is over. Ninth grade feels so long ago. The question for all of us is, What's next? Some of us will work. Some of us will travel. Some of us are going to schools far away. I got a scholarship to my top university. And it scares me. What if I fail? I always find a way...a way to what?

Buzz buzz

Hey, Myles.

<Attachment>

"What the fuck?"

Hellllooooooo?

Who is this?

Just call me O.

Where did you get this picture?

This could be a big problem for you.
Don't you think?

...

What, no snappy comeback, wonder
boy?

Who IS this?

So Myles was at THAT party? The
rugby one? Where those poor
freshmen were hazed?

Is this Danny? Why are you doing this?

That's right. Danny was one. And
there were 2 more. What were their
names?

Danny, this is not funny.

I am not Danny. My name is O.

Is this a joke? Why are you doing this?

I guess you don't remember. Let me help you.

Where did you get this picture?

You lied, Myles. You said you weren't there that night. Which is strange. Wouldn't the captain of the rugby team be at the rugby party? But you said you didn't go. Lucky Myles. Your friends were not so lucky. Declan. Viraj. Mike. They got kicked out of school. But not Myles. Because wonder boy wasn't there. Smart, cool, dependable Myles. Let's take a look at that pic again.

<Attachment>

What do you want from me?

What will everyone think when they find out you lied?

What do you WANT?

I want to play.

This isn't a game! This is my life you're messing with.

Ah, but it is a game, wonder boy. My game. So listen up. I have planned a little scavenger hunt for you. If you can find all the items, I will give you the image file.

What if I can't?

Well, grad is in 6 hours. If you don't complete my game by then...

Then what?

11

Then I'll post the picture online. And everyone will know the truth. Better hurry, Myles. Your future is at stake.

...

Hello?

What do I have to do?

St. Mark's Elementary School. Parking lot. Good luck, wonder boy.

Chapter Two

OK. I'm at the school. Now what?

 …

HELLO?!

 No need to shout.

I'm at St. Mark's.

 That was fast. I didn't think you had
 a car.

I don't. I ran.

Ha ha. Wow. I guess you really do want

this file.

Would you stop screwing around? I did

what you told me to. I'm following the rules.

What's next?

You went to this school. As a kid.

Yeah. Did you?

I ask the questions, wonder boy. You

went here. So did Declan.

Yeah, so?

And Mike. And Viraj. See that wall?

The one with the basketball nets?

You played a lot of ball here.

You seem to know a lot about us. I think

you went to St. Mark's too.

If you say so. And over there. By the

soccer nets. That's where Viraj broke

his arm. You ran for help. You were in second grade. Little kids.

What's your point?

You were friends here.

That was a long time ago.

A long time since you were a little kid. Not since you were friends.

Things change.

They sure do. Pretty easy to ditch your friends, Myles. They get into trouble and BAM! Myles is gone. So much for loyalty.

Declan? Is this you? We talked about this. You know why I had to lie.

Ha ha. Come on, wonder boy. Do you think Declan could put this game together? He's way too busy doing—what's he doing these days?

You said this was a game. What do you want me to do?

Do you remember Maddie Bobek? She was in your class.

What about her?

Remember that time in third grade? When she peed her pants?

You know about that? Yeah, you definitely went to St. Mark's.

Why did she pee her pants, Myles?

...

Come on, Myles. I know you remember. She was scared. Scared that she lost her...

Maddie? Is this Maddie?

Oh, I wish. Maddie is the best. Now

answer me. Maddie was scared because she lost her what?

Bear. She lost her teddy bear.

That's right. Someone stole it. And hid it.

It was just a joke. I didn't know she would be so upset.

Where did you hide the bear?

I don't know! It was a long time ago! I was a kid!

Well, you'd better figure it out. Because that's where your next clue is. Tick-tock, wonder boy.

———

Gemma! Babe! Do you have Maddie Bobek's number?

Maddie Bobek? Random. What do you need her number for?

...

Myles?

For my speech. I just need to ask her something.

OK. I just sent you her contact info.

...

Myles?

Hello?

———

Maddie? Are you doing this?

Who is this?

It's Myles. Are you the one who's been texting me?

What? You texted me! Myles...Myles King?

Yeah. Sorry. Just...got a weird text.

OK...

I just...listen, I...uh...I'm sorry.

I don't get it. You're sorry for texting me?

No. I was writing my speech for tonight. Just remembered some stuff. From grade school.

St. Mark's? That was forever ago.

Yeah. But I just...I'm sorry. About the bear.

...

...

It was really mean of me.

Thanks, Myles. I appreciate that.

...

Did you ever find it?

Yeah. Well, Jess Pineda did. Under the portable. How did you even get under there?

I was pretty scrawny back then...and a jerk.

You were.

...

Hey good luck tonight. At grad.

Thanks, Maddie.

———

Did you find it?

Yes.

What did you find?

A teddy bear. Like Maddie's bear. It's
holding a note that says Lake Central Park.
That's all the way across town.

Better hurry, wonder boy.

Chapter Three

Where are you? I went to the school.
Brought you some lunch. You weren't
there.

...

Answer me, young man.

Sorry, Mom. I went for a run.

A run? In your jeans?

Yeah. Needed to clear my head.

Where are you now?

Lake Central Park.

The lake? That's a long way.

It's fine, Mom.

Where at the park? I'll swing by. Drop off your lunch.

No. I'm still running.

You must be hungry.

I brought granola bars.

That's not a real lunch.

Mom, please! I just need to be alone!

Is everything ok?

...

Myles?

I'm fine, Mom. Don't worry so much.

Jax! I need your help. Have you heard from Declan?

I thought you didn't want to talk about Declan.

It's important.

No. I haven't heard from him. That's why I asked you. I'm worried about him.

What about Mike? Or Viraj?

I talked to Viraj a couple days ago. He said Declan is acting weird. Depressed or something. He didn't know. That's why I was worried.

Acting weird how?

Not like himself. Viraj said he doesn't answer his phone. Like at all.

His phone…

Why are you asking? You told me never to talk about those guys.

I know. It's just…did Viraj say anything about me?

No.

Like about being mad at me?

No. Why?

Did he say if Declan was mad at me?

Because you stopped talking to him?

Myles, what is going on?

Nothing. Never mind.

You could text Declan. He'd probably like to hear from you. You guys were close.

Yeah, maybe I will. Thanks, Jax.

———

Declan? You there?

...

I don't know if this is still your number. You around?

———

Are you at the park yet?

Yes. What do I have to do now?

Wow. Super speedy. You really are an athlete. I can see why you got that scholarship.

My grades helped.

Sure. You're very successful, Myles. It would be a shame if it all went away.

Stop trying to scare me.

You should be scared, Myles. One little picture. But you know if it gets uploaded to social media…that's IT for you.

I don't understand. Did I do something to you? Why are you doing this?

Because someone has to, Myles. Someone has to teach you. You have to learn.

Learn what?

That you're not special. That you don't just get everything you want. No one does.

Declan, if this is you, I'm sorry. I talked to Jax. I know things haven't been great since you got kicked out of school.

Ha ha. Back on the Declan theory?
It's not Declan. Stop trying to figure
out who I am. I told you who I am.
I am O. That's all you need to know.
And right now, you are wasting time.
I left you a present.

Where?

Let's see if you can guess. You come
here a lot. Don't you, Myles?

It's Lake Central Park. Everyone comes here.

Right. Everyone who's anyone. You
can't be nobody. You have to be
somebody.

What are you talking about?

When did the cool kids start coming
here? Ninth grade? Great place to
smoke. Get high.

I don't smoke.

> Of course not. Not wonder boy. But other cool people do. Have to be cool though. Not like Adam Oakley.

OK, I get your point.

> Do you?

I was a dick to Adam Oakley in ninth grade. I'm sorry. I'm an asshole.

> What did you do to Adam Oakley?

Are you Adam Oakley?

> No. LOL. Tell me what you did.

I didn't let him hang out with us. He showed up at the park. No one invited him. And I laughed at him. It was a shitty thing to do. I shouldn't have. It was a long time ago.

> Maddie was a long time ago.

OK. You've made your point. I'm the worst.

Got it. Do you want me to say sorry to Oakley? Give me his number. I'll call him right now.

> I don't have his number. And I doubt he'd want to hear from you. Adam Oakley hates you.

Are YOU Adam Oakley? Does O stand for Oakley?

> No. What happened to Adam Oakley that night?

Everyone knows.

> I don't.

I think you do.

> Tell me anyway.

He fell off the pier. Landed in the lake. It was April, so the lake was really cold. He had to go to the hospital. Get treated for

hypothermia. He was fine though. He was back at school on Monday.

He FELL, Myles?

…

Myles?

He jumped off. We dared him to jump.

We?

Me and Declan.

Whose idea was it?

Both of ours.

Someone came up with it first.

I can't remember.

Sure you can.

Me. It was me. Are you happy now?

Very good, Myles. Your next clue is waiting where Oakley jumped.

On the pier?

...

O? Hello?

———

I'm on the pier. I don't see anything.

> It's not on the pier, silly. I said where
> Oakley jumped.

Like in the water?

> Gosh, you are smart.

Are you insane? I'm not jumping in there.

> Why not? It's June. The water is warm
> enough.

**And what? Swim to the bottom? Even if I
could get down there, I can't see anything.**

> Sure you can. Look for a neon orange
> bag. I'm sure you'll see it.

You're crazy.

And you're running out of time. Don't forget the rules of the game, wonder boy. Win or lose. The choice is yours.

Chapter Four

Jax, can you bring me some clothes?

Clothes? What do you mean, man?

I fell in the lake. I need dry clothes.

THE LAKE!? I thought you were at school? Writing your speech?

I'm in trouble, Jax.

What kind of trouble?

Someone's messing with me.

Who?

I don't know. Declan maybe? Or Viraj or Mike?

Is that why you were asking about them?

Or Oakley maybe? I don't know! But things are getting out of hand.

What do you mean? Wait, is that why you ended up in the lake?

Yeah. Jax, I need your help. I'm soaked. And I have to get to the graveyard behind Big Burger. Can you pick me up?

What's going on?

I'll tell you when you get here. Just bring me some clothes. And hurry.

On my way.

———

I'm at the graveyard.

You jumped in the lake?

I did.

Wow. I didn't think you would do it. So what did you find?

Your orange bag. With the Big Burger wrapper. And a candle.

And what does that mean?

Go to the graveyard.

How do you know that?

Because the wrapper is for the burger place. And the candle is for Leah.

What about her?

Save it, O. I'm not doing this. I don't know how you know about Leah. Maybe you're friends with her.

Or maybe I AM Leah?

She wouldn't do this.

Because you know her so well.

What happened between me and Leah is between us. So just shut up. I'm not getting into all that. Not with you. I found the next clue. I'm on my way to the train station.

Where did you find it?

In the graveyard. Like I said.

Where in the graveyard?

Whoever you are, this is sick. I don't know how you know all this stuff about me. About my past.

Where in the graveyard, Myles?

I'm going to the train.

Jack Dawson's grave, right? Like Leo in Titanic? Was that where you found my clue? You think I'M sick? LOL

You're the guy who lost his virginity over a grave. Who does that?

It wasn't like we planned it! It just happened! It was a Halloween thing. A seance. We were trying to contact the dead. It was Leah's idea.

Talking to ghosts. Pretty hot. Whatever turns you on, I guess.

It's none of your business!

You're right. It's none of my business. I didn't mean to upset you. I bet Leah didn't either.

Shut up.

Is that why you ghosted her? Ha ha. Ghosted. That's funny.

...

Well? You stopped answering her texts. Stopped talking to her at school. Pretty cold, bro.

Leah's my friend. I don't know what she told you. But we're friends.

Are you sure about that? She trusted you.

I trusted her too.

What's that supposed to mean?

She laughed at me, OK? Did Leah tell you that? When we were together. Our first time. During. She laughed at me. I was embarrassed. I couldn't face her after that. It was immature. I know that. But I was humiliated. Why are you making me talk about this? It was forever ago.

We put it behind us. We are friends now. So just forget it.

I'm sorry your feelings were hurt.

But you're still an asshole.

I know that.

What did you find?

What?

At Jack Dawson's grave. What did you find?

A train ticket and a key. I'm not getting on a train.

Then you won't win the game.

Grad is in like, three hours!

And your train leaves in 15 minutes.

Tick-tock, wonder boy.

Chapter Five

Did you make the train?

Yeah. It was close. But I made it. I'm on the train. Thanks for the ride, Jax.

I almost wish you'd missed it. I don't like this, Myles. That graveyard thing was crazy. And jumping in the lake? The person doing this—I'm scared for you. What do they want?

I don't know. I guess I'll find out when I get to the city.

> I don't mean the train, man. I mean what do they want from you? Why are they doing this?

I told you. They want to ruin my life.

> But how? Why can't you just ignore the texts?

I can't ignore them. My whole future is riding on it.

> HOW though? What are you not telling me?

Just trust me. If I don't play O's game, my life is over. Please don't make me say more.

> OK. I just want to help.

You can help by going over to Oakley's house.

I'll head there now. But I don't think it's Oakley. He's a pretty laid-back guy. Is there anyone else it could be?

Maybe. I am still thinking Declan or those other guys are involved.

I told you. Viraj didn't mention you. That story about Leah was pretty personal. How many people did you tell about it?

Just you.

Are you sure there was no one else? Not even Declan? Or Gemma?

No.

Could it be one of Leah's friends?

Like who? Daisy and Carmen? They aren't like that. You know them better than I do. Besides, they didn't go to St. Mark's.

St. Mark's? The elementary school?

Yeah. Whoever is doing this, they know a lot about St. Mark's.

Declan went to St. Mark's. Did he ever respond to your text?

No.

Try him again. I'll update you when I'm done talking to Oakley.

OK. And Jax...thanks for your help.

Anytime.

———

Hey babe. How's the speech going?

OK. Almost done.

Sweet! What time are you picking me up?

Picking you up?

For grad. You said you'd pick me up.

Oh. Can't you go with your parents?

Um...wow.

I'm sorry. I'm just really stressed out. I have to finish this speech. I have to go home and shower. And change. And there's just a lot to do. I don't know if I'll have time. It's just for the ceremony. I'll take you to Rich's party after. Is that OK?

I guess...

Gem, I'm sorry. This has been a really bad day. I'm trying.

All right.

Please don't be mad.

...

Chapter Six

What do you want, Myles?

Declan! You got my texts?

Yes. What do you want?

Are you mad at me or something?

Mad about what?

About what happened. About the rugby party.

At you?

Yeah.

Why are you asking? It's been months. You haven't talked to me since I got kicked out. And now you're wondering if I'm mad?

Yes.

You did what you had to do, Myles. I get it. You're the golden boy. Honor roll. Valedictorian. Team captain. You were always the good guy. And I'm the bad guy.

I'm not always the good guy.

That's right, you're not. But no one else seems to know that.

I know it. Especially today.

Whatever. It doesn't change what happened. I started the hazing. You stopped it. You were right. I screwed up. I get that. I have to pay for it. And I accept that. That's all I can do. Take responsibility for my actions. So I am.

But you're still mad.

I'm not mad at you for doing the right thing, Myles.

Then why are you mad?

You ditched me. I know I screwed up. That's on me. But you just stopped talking to me. As soon as they kicked us out, it was like we were dead to you. You never even TRIED to talk about what happened. We've been best friends since kindergarten. Do you have any idea how hard these last few months have been for me? I'm not going to college. I'm not even graduating. I'm working at the deli. My clothes stink of meat all day. Every day. No one from school talks to me. It's been hell, Myles. And my best friend doesn't even care.

I should have called.

You think?

Is that why you are doing this?

Doing what?

Teaching me a lesson?

What are you talking about?

I'm on the train.

What train? Isn't grad tonight?

Declan, no more bullshit. Are you the one doing this?

Doing what? What the hell are you
talking about?

———

Are you on the train?

Yeah.

Good. Get off at Union. Do you see
the number on the key?

Yeah. 7725. Is this a station locker?

So smart, wonder boy. Text when
you arrive.

———

Myles? Hello!?!?!? What's going on?

**Nothing. Decs, I'm sorry. I'm sorry I didn't
call. I should have. Really. I mean that.
When the party was in the newspaper...**

and the police got involved...I got scared.

I got really scared, Decs.

> Why were you scared? You didn't do
> anything wrong.

I was there.

> Yeah, you were. But you made us stop.
> You broke it up.

I told the cops I wasn't there.

> I know.

You never told them I was there?

> They told me you said you weren't
> there. So I just...agreed. You were so
> freaked about losing your scholarship.
> I didn't want you to lose it either.

**I should have told them I was there. I've
messed everything up.**

Myles, I messed everything up. Viraj messed up. And Mike. You didn't.

I lied.

You had your reasons.

Yeah...I'm starting to think they weren't good ones. I should have talked to you. I owed you that. And I'm sorry.

It's fine. It's been a rough year for both of us.

...

Myles? Are you OK?

...

No. I don't think so.

Can I help?

You ever use a storage locker at Union Station?

Yeah. Once. With you. My brother left our Bile tickets in one of those lockers. Last summer. Remember? He couldn't meet us on time. He had to work. So he left our tickets in a locker.

Oh yeah. We picked them up before the concert.

Why are you asking about storage lockers?

No reason. Thanks, Decs.

Sure.

———

Are you downtown yet?

Hey, Jax. Yeah. I'm off the train.

I talked to Oakley. It's not him. He just got back from Ottawa. He's been moving into a student house there. Gone all week. There's no way he could have set all this up.

No, I know it's not Oakley. I just talked to Declan.

Is it him?

No. But he reminded me of something. I'm getting a train home now.

Did you get to the locker?

No. I'm not going.

Why not?

Because I know who's doing this. And I'm ending it.

Who is it?

I'll tell you when I see you.

> Myles, grad is in like one hour. You're
> not going to be back in time.

I'll make it. I'm getting on the train now.
See you soon.

Chapter Seven

Did you find the locker?

No.

Tick-tock, wonder boy. Grad is in 45
minutes. You might not make it.

I know what's in the locker.

I doubt that.

I do, Lara.

...

What makes you think I'm Lara?

Declan. I talked to him. He reminded me about the time I went to the Bile concert. That was the day I was supposed to be at your house. We had a physics project due the next day.

I'm surprised you remember.

I left you to do all the work. That was not cool. I shouldn't have done that. I remember how mad you were. I blew you off. We got a bad mark. It was my fault. Sure. I get that. 60% isn't the best. But is it really worth all this?

Do you know what that 60% did to my mark? Do you know what my physics grade did to my school options? I was supposed to go to McGill! 60%, Myles!

For me, it might as well have been a ZERO!!!!!

That's why you call yourself O. It's not a letter. It's a number. A zero.

That's right, wonder boy. If I had been named valedictorian, that might have helped. They might have overlooked the grade. But you had to take that from me too.

And that's what was in the locker. Our paper. With the grade.

Very good, Myles. You figured it out. You are smarter than I thought. But that doesn't change anything.

What do you mean?

You didn't play by the rules. You lost, Myles. Game over.

Oh please. You were never going to let me win. A game made up of your rules. You made sure I couldn't win.

> Right again. Wonder Boy Myles. Gets everything he wants. Not today. After everything you've done? To Maddie? To Adam? To Leah? Not to mention Declan, Mike and Viraj. I'm tired of people not seeing what kind of person you really are. It's time they knew.

And then what? It won't change the mark, Lara. It won't make you valedictorian.

> Probably not. But it will still feel good.

Fine. If I have to lose, I'm losing my way.

> What does that mean?

See you at grad, Lara.

OMG Lara! Did you see this?

<Attachment>

Where did you get this, Carmen?

Myles just posted it! Everyone's freaking. He's supposed to give a speech in like, 10 minutes. Why would he do that?

I...I don't know.

I just saw his mom and sister. Don't see him anywhere. Are you at school yet?

Almost.

I just can't get over it. Didn't he say he wasn't at the rugby party? I always thought he was lying. Him and Declan went everywhere together. What a day to confess.

Yeah...pretty bizarre.

Wait! I see him! He just walked in.
OMG, he's a total mess.

What do you mean?

He's in like, jeans that are too big for
him. And an old T-shirt. His hair is
crazy. Like he just went swimming.
Is this what a nervous breakdown
looks like? You gotta get here! You
can't miss this!

I just pulled in. I'll find you in the
gym.

He's getting on the podium. I think
he's going to give his speech. I wonder
what he's going to say?

Should be interesting.

Oh wow. Looks like he just posted his speech too. Right under that picture. Check it out.

Here we are. High school is over. Ninth grade feels so long ago. The question for all of us is, What's next? Some of us will work. Some of us will travel. Some of us are going to schools far away. I got a scholarship to my first-choice university. And it scares me. What if I fail?

I didn't know how to finish this speech. Didn't know how to face failure. What if I fail? What if? I spent all day trying to answer that question. Because the truth is, failure has never been an option for me. I work hard. I try hard. Because I am trying not to fail. What would it say about me if I failed at something? But the thing is, sometimes failure happens. We fall short of who we want to be—or who we think we are. We make mistakes. We mess up. We hurt people. So what do we do then? Get back up, they tell us. Try again. People always say that. Get back up. Just try again. It's easy to say...if you've never been knocked down. I got knocked down today. Again. And again. And again. Lower than I've ever been. And I could have stayed down. Because when you're on the ground, you can see how far you've fallen. And all the people you've knocked down on the way. Sometimes you didn't mean to. Sometimes you did. But all those people that were down on the ground because of you? They aren't there anymore. Because they got back up. They kept trying. Kept striving. And I realized I wanted to be like them. Wanted to be brave.

Like all of you. Strong enough to get back up. And try again.

So here I am. Back on my feet. And it's scary. I have to take responsibility for what I've done. That's part of growing up, isn't it? Taking responsibility. Even if it means doing something scary. Even if it means not getting what we want. Even if it means failing. Because sometimes there's no avoiding failure. So to come back to the question, What if I fail? What if you fail? Then we fail. But here's something I know now. We will always, always get back up. And then we'll try again.

Epilogue

Six Months Later

Hey, Myles.

Well if it isn't O. Been a while. How's Western treating you?

Yeah, school's been really busy. Exams nearly killed me.

Sure.

Anyway, I'm home now.

For the holidays?

Yeah.

Good for you.

So…my mom said she saw you at Antonio's. You work there now?

Yeah, it's all right. I get a lot of free pizza. So that's good.

She told me you got your scholarship back.

Yeah. After the fallout from grad, the university revoked it. But then Declan talked to Principal Stevens. Told them what happened at the rugby party. Viraj and Mike spoke up too.

That was nice of them.

Yeah, Principal Stevens talked to the dean at Queens. There was a lot of back and forth. Took forever.

And?

And I start next fall.

That's awesome, Myles.

Yeah, I guess it all worked out.

I feel like I should say I'm sorry. About everything.

But you're not. I get it.

So why didn't you ever tell anyone? About O?

Did you want me to?

No. I just...don't understand why you didn't rat me out.

What's the point? You were right. I was an asshole.

So was I.

Well...O was

I guess.

Hey, Gem's coming home tonight too. We were going to meet up with Jax and Oakley at Antonio's for pizza. You want to join?

Really?

Yeah. Why not?

OK. That's cool of you, Myles.

Well I am the Wonder Boy.

All right. Shut up.

😊

Has Jaylin received a message from beyond the grave?

"An edge-of-the-seat experience."
—*CM Reviews*

Eshana discovers a website that grants wishes, but is having the life she's always wanted worth the cost?

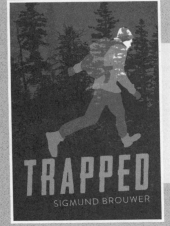

Matt makes a startling discovery that he hides from his abusive foster parents.

"Taut and gripping."
—*Kirkus Reviews*

M.J. McIsaac is the author of several books for young people, including *Boil Line* and *Underhand* in the Orca Sports line and the Orca Currents title *Alien Road*. She has a master's degree in writing for children and is an accomplished illustrator as well. She lives with her family in Whitby, Ontario.

For more information on all the books

in the Orca Anchor line, please visit

orcabook.com